STO

DO NOT REMOVE
CARDS FROM POCKET

3/94

ONE LITTLE MONKEY
To librarians, parents, and teachers:

One Little Monkey is a Parents Magazine READ
ALOUD Original — one title in a series of colorfully
illustrated and fun-to-read stories that young readers
will be sure to come back to time and time again.

Now, in this special school and library edition of
One Little Monkey, adults have an even greater
opportunity to increase children's responsiveness to
reading and learning — and to have fun every step of
the way.

When you finish this story, check the special section
at the back of the book. There you will find games,
projects, things to talk about, and other educational
activities designed to make reading enjoyable by
giving children and adults a chance to play together,
work together, and talk over the story they have
just read.

For a free color catalog describing Gareth Stevens' list of high-quality books, call 1-800-341-3569 (USA) or 1-800-461-9120 (Canada).

Parents Magazine READ ALOUD Originals:

Golly Gump Swallowed a Fly	Henry's Important Date
The Housekeeper's Dog	Elephant Goes to School
Who Put the Pepper in the Pot?	Rabbit's New Rug
Those Terrible Toy-Breakers	Sand Cake
The Ghost in Dobbs Diner	Socks for Supper
The Biggest Shadow in the Zoo	The Clown-Arounds Go on Vacation
The Old Man and the Afternoon Cat	The Little Witch Sisters
Septimus Bean and His Amazing Machine	The Very Bumpy Bus Ride
Sherlock Chick's First Case	Henry Babysits
A Garden for Miss Mouse	There's No Place Like Home
Witches Four	Up Goes Mr. Downs
Bread and Honey	Bicycle Bear
Pigs in the House	Sweet Dreams, Clown-Arounds!
Milk and Cookies	The Man Who Cooked for Himself
But No Elephants	Where's Rufus?
No Carrots for Harry!	The Giggle Book
Snow Lion	Pickle Things
Henry's Awful Mistake	Oh, So Silly!
The Fox with Cold Feet	The Peace-and-Quiet Diner
Get Well, Clown-Arounds!	Ten Furry Monsters
Pets I Wouldn't Pick	One Little Monkey
Sherlock Chick and the Giant	The Silly Tail Book
Egg Mystery	Aren't You Forgetting Something, Fiona?
Cats! Cats! Cats!	

Library of Congress Cataloging-in-Publication Data

Calmenson, Stephanie.
    One little monkey/ by Stephanie Calmenson; pictures by Ellen Appleby.
      p. cm. — (Parents magazine read aloud original)
    "North American library edition"—T.p. verso.
    Summary: Swinging through the trees in the jungle because he's been stung by a bee, one monkey is followed by groups of animals from two to ten who think hunters must be pursuing them.
    ISBN 0-8368-0988-2
    [1. Animals—Fiction. 2. Jungles—Fiction. 3. Counting. 4. Stories in rhyme.] I. Appleby, Ellen, ill. II. Title.   III. Series.
    PZ8.3.C130n 1994
    [E]—dc20   93-36141

This North American library edition published in 1994 by Gareth Stevens Publishing, 1555 North RiverCenter Drive, Suite 201, Milwaukee, Wisconsin 53212, USA, under an arrangement with Parents Magazine Press, New York.

Text © 1982 by Stephanie Calmenson. Illustrations © 1982 by Ellen Appleby. Portions of end matter adapted from material first published in the newsletter *From Parents to Parents* by the Parents Magazine Read Aloud Book Club, © 1988 by Gruner + Jahr, USA, Publishing; other portions © 1994 by Gareth Stevens, Inc.

Printed in the United States of America

1 2 3 4 5 6 7 8 9 99 98 97 96 95 94

ONE LITTLE MONKEY

by **Stephanie Calmenson**
pictures by **Ellen Appleby**

Gareth Stevens Publishing
Milwaukee
Parents Magazine Press
New York

For Mom and Dad
and Michael—S.C.

To my mother,
for all her help—E.A.

One little monkey
Sitting in a tree
Got stung on the tail
By a buzzing bumble bee.

8

The monkey started swinging
As fast as he could go.
Two hippos saw him racing by
And shouted from below,

"Is there trouble in the jungle?"
"Yes there is, indeed!"

So the hippos started running
At breakneck speed.

Now just behind the hippos
Three zebras stood out grazing.
And when they saw those hippos run
They thought it was amazing.

"It sure must be important,"
Said Zebra Number Three.
"I guess we'd better follow them.
Stay very close to me!"

The zebras started running
As quickly as they could
And passed four lively antelope
Playing in the wood.

"The hunters must be coming!
We can't waste any time."
And so they followed after
The quickly growing line.

There were monkey, hippos, zebras,
Antelope, and then
They ran into five lions
Roaring in their den.

"It has to be the hunters!"
Said the smallest one.
So they stopped what they were doing
And broke into a run.

"A game of tag?" said Big Baboon.
"Will you let us play?"
"No, no! It's hunters," Lion said.
And six baboons were on their way.

A herd of sleepy elephants
Cried, "Danger must be near!"

So seven husky elephants
Followed to the rear.

Eight parrots singing in a tree
Saw the herd pass by.
"It must be time to leave the nest!"
Then they began to fly.

Nine giraffes were eating lunch,
a meal of tasty leaves.

They heard the call to come along
And they caught up with ease.

Ten tigers playing leapfrog
Quickly took the hint.
"We *thought* we smelled some hunters."
And they began to sprint.

They had not traveled very far...

When everyone stopped short.
"Oh, no!" cried all the animals.
"Did someone just get caught?"

37

"Why are you stopping, monkey?
The hunters must be near.
And they are sure to catch us
If we are standing here!"

The monkey started laughing.
"There are no hunters — see?
I only had my tail stung
By a buzzing bumble bee."

But while the monkey laughed at them
The others turned and then —
Uh-oh, Little Monkey...

HO HO
HEE HEE

You just got stung again!

Notes to Grown-ups

Major Themes

Here is a quick guide to the significant themes and concepts at work in *One Little Monkey:*

- Don't follow anyone unless you know why: the animals ran just because they saw the others running. They didn't try to find out what was really going on.
- Enjoy counting: this is a counting book with rhymes and pictures to add to the fun.

Step-by-step Ideas for Reading and Talking

Here are some ideas for further give-and-take between grown-ups and children. The following topics encourage creative discussion of *One Little Monkey* and invite the kind of open-ended response that is consistent with many contemporary approaches to reading, including Whole Language:

- Identify the animals in the book. Note that these animals live in a jungle. What kind of place is the jungle to live? Is it warm or cold? What is there for the animals to eat? Talk about other places animals may live. For example, what animals live on a farm? In a desert? In the Arctic?
- Talk about major and minor characters. The bee and the monkey are important because they set off the action. The animals that run after the monkey are important because they move the story along. Other animals only watch. Which ones are they?
- Rhymes help children listen to the sounds of words and eventually speak more clearly. As you read you can stress the rhymes. Point out some of the rhyming pairs, such as three/me, then/den, and play/way.

Games for Learning

Games and activities can stimulate young readers and listeners alike to find out more about words, numbers, and ideas. Here are more ideas for turning learning into fun:

Count Those Animals!

If you would like to help your child learn number names and concepts, this book can be a great resource. After you've read it through once for fun, go through it again and have your child hold up the correct number of fingers for each new group of animals on the run.

Variations:

To see how many animals actually stampede to the pond and to reinforce one-to-one correspondence (matching number names with the correct number of objects counted), help your child count out the same number of beans or cereal as there are animals on each page as they are introduced. Put them in a bowl as you go. When you get to the end of the story, you will have only counted to ten, but there will be many more than ten beans in the bowl. Why is that? Help your child go back and look at the pictures to discover the answer.

This story also reveals what can happen when one small incident occurs. To extend this concept, ask your child to tell you what might happen if:
- you poured the last bit of cereal into your bowl but then accidentally spilled it all over the floor.
- you left a red crayon in the pocket of your white shorts and the shorts accidentally got washed with the whole family's white clothes.

About the Author

STEPHANIE CALMENSON says she wanted to write a story about Little Monkey as soon as she saw the monkey that Ellen Appleby had drawn in her sketchbook. "It's fun making up stories that way," she says.

In fact, the author hopes the children who read this book might select one of the animals in it and make up a story of their own.

Stephanie Calmenson has written and edited many books for children. She lives in New York City.

About the Artist

ELLEN APPLEBY lives and works in New York City. To draw the animals in this book, she wanted real-life models. So she walked over to the Central Park Zoo, where monkeys, hippos, zebras, and many other jungle animals live.

Ellen Appleby is a graduate of the Rhode Island School of Design. Her favorite animal is her dog, Nancy, a large Airedale terrier.